Bordaria
Difendere con Coraggio

Scholastic Canada Ltd.
604 King Street West, Toronto, Ontario M5V 1E1, Canada

Scholastic Inc.
557 Broadway, New York, NY 10012, USA

Scholastic Australia Pty Limited
PO Box 579, Gosford, NSW 2250, Australia

Scholastic New Zealand Limited
Private Bag 94407, Botany, Manukau 2163, New Zealand

Scholastic Children's Books
Euston House, 24 Eversholt Street, London NW1 1DB, UK

www.scholastic.ca

PÖP & FÍZZ

Published by Pop & Fizz and Scholastic Australia in 2010.
Pop & Fizz is a partnership between Paddlepop Press and Lemonfizz Media.
www.paddlepoppress.com
Text, design and illustrations copyright © Lemonfizz Media 2010.
Cover illustration by Melanie Matthews.
Internal illustrations by Lionel Portier, Melanie Matthews, Steve Karp and James Hart

First published by Scholastic Australia in 2010.
This edition published by Scholastic Canada Ltd. in 2013.

Library and Archives Canada Cataloguing in Publication

Park, Mac

Isolus / Mac Park.

(Boy vs beast. Battle of the borders)

ISBN 978-1-4431-1904-7

I. Title. II. Series: Park, Mac. Boy vs. beast. Battle of the borders.

PZ7.P2213Is 2013   j823'.92   C2012-905212-4

6 5 4 3 2 1   Printed in Canada 139   13 14 15 16

BOY vs BEAST

BATTLE OF THE BORDERS

ISOLUS

Mac Park

POP & F!ZZ

SCHOLASTIC

Prologue

Long ago beast and man shared one world. Then battles began between them.

After many battles, the world was split in two. Beasts were given Beastium. Man was given Earth.

A border-wall was made. It closed the two worlds off.

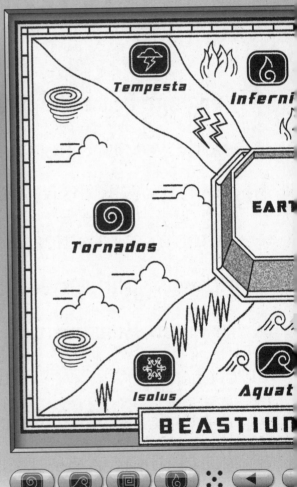

Tempesta

Inferni

Tornados

EART

Isolus

Aquat

BEASTIUM

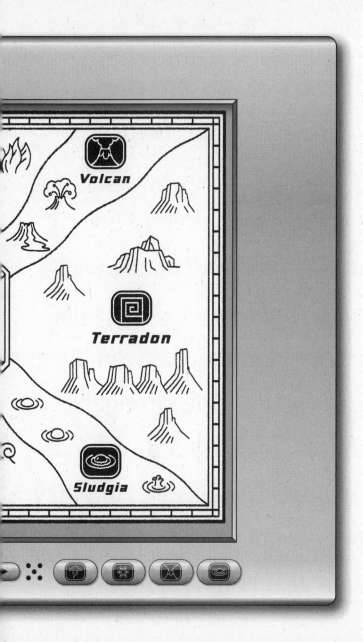

Volcan

Terradon

Sludgia

Border Guards were trained to defend the border-wall.

The beasts tried to get through the border-wall many times. The Border Guards had to stop them. Battles won by beasts made them stronger. Battles won by guards earned them new battle gear. And they got new upgrades. Then their battle gear could do more.

Five boys now defend the border-wall. They are in training to become Border Masters. Just like their dads.

Their dads were also Border Guards once. Then they became Border Captains and then Border Knights. They kept learning until they became Border Masters. Now they make up the Bordaria Master Command. The BMC.

The BMC helped the Border Guards during battle. They gave the Border Guards new battle gear.

The boys had to earn new battle gear. They needed to learn from their battles and from their mistakes.

Kai Masters is a Border Guard. His work is top secret. The BMC watch Kai closely. Kai must not fail.

The Beastium Border-Lands

The beasts of Beastium lived in four lands. There was a fire land. There was a rock land and a water land. And there was an air land.

But over time, the edges of the lands mixed. That was how the border-lands were made.

The edges of fire and rock mixed. That made a volcano land. The edges of rock and water mixed. That made a mud border-land.

The edges of water and wind mixed. That made an ice border-land. The edges of wind and fire mixed. That made a storm border-land.

But it was not just the edges of the worlds that mixed.

The beasts from each of the worlds mixed, too. And then a new kind of beast was made . . .

The border-land beast.

Kai Masters must think about his old battles. He must learn from them. If he does not, then he will fail.

Kai must not lose.

Chapter 1

It was a hot summer day.
Kai Masters was playing
baseball. He was at the field.
And he was really hot. Kai's hair
was wet under his cap.

The game was almost over.
Kai was off to the beach after
the game.

I can't wait to go for a

swim, thought Kai. *Only one ball to go.* It was Kai's turn to bat. He held the bat up. He was ready to hit the ball. Then he felt something cold on his arms. It was snow! It was falling from the sky.

Soon there was snow everywhere. All the kids began playing in it. Everyone was throwing snowballs. Everyone but Kai.

Kai Masters was a Border Guard. It was his job to keep Earth safe. Safe from beasts that tried to break through the border-wall. It was Kai's job to know when things weren't right.

Snow in the middle of summer? thought Kai. He took out his pocket compass. Kai looked at where the snow was coming from. *The compass*

shows it's from the south,
thought Kai. *A beast from the*
water land might be doing this.

Just then Kai's orbix beeped.
Every Border Guard had an orb.
It could be used for lots of
things.

The BMC used the orb to
talk with Kai. And sometimes
so did BC3. But only when he
was not with Kai. BC had sent
Kai a message.

When are we
going to the
beach? BC

BC was Kai's robotic dog.
The BMC gave him to Kai as a
prize. BC helped Kai in battle.
And he was good fun at the
beach. Kai wrote back to BC.

Snow at the field. Not good.

No beach today ☹

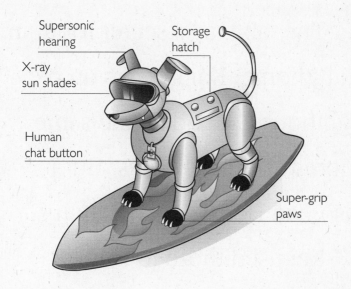

Supersonic hearing

Storage hatch

X-ray sun shades

Human chat button

Super-grip paws

Kai opened the orb. He put some snow inside it. He shut the orb and set it to chill.

I need to get this to the lab, thought Kai.

The lab was a secret room in Kai's home. Kai lived in an old lighthouse. It had all the same rooms as other homes. But it also had Border Guard rooms.

Kai used these to learn about beasts. And to get ready for battle.

Kai put the orb in his pocket. Then he jumped on his bike. He rode up the hill fast. Up the hill to the lighthouse.

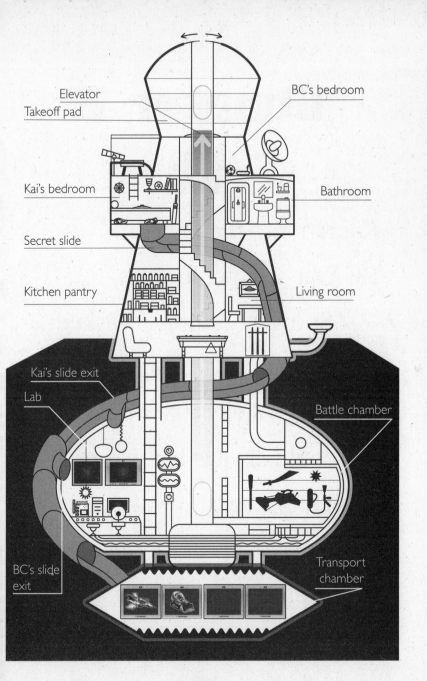

Elevator

Takeoff pad

BC's bedroom

Kai's bedroom

Bathroom

Secret slide

Kitchen pantry

Living room

Kai's slide exit

Lab

Battle chamber

BC's slide exit

Transport chamber

Chapter 2

Kai ran into the kitchen.

BC was waiting for him.

"Snow in summer?" asked

BC. His tail was wagging.

That was always bad news.

BC could always tell when

something beastly was going on.

"Yes," said Kai. "I have some

in the orb. We need to test it in

the lab. Come on BC, let's go."

Kai went into the kitchen pantry. He pressed the button under the bottom shelf.
The back wall of the pantry began to move. There was a ladder behind the wall. Kai and BC climbed down it into the lab.

Kai put the snow into the tester. He turned the computer on. The computer screen flashed.

"The water land and the wind land," said Kai. "I feel cold just thinking about it."

Kai watched the screen and waited. Then the screen flashed again.

"That land is freezing!"
said BC.

"Yes," said Kai. "It's an ice
land." Kai pushed a button.
A card popped up on the
screen.

BEAST I.D.

CHILLMINITAN

This snowball fight is no game

Strength	★★★★★
Attack Power	★★★★★
Speed	★★★★★

"We'll need to heat things up. That's how we'll stop that beast," said Kai. "Time to pick our battle gear, BC."

Kai took out his Border Guard Card. He put it into the computer slot. He heard a noise he knew well.

CLUNK! BANG! Whiiiiir! BANG!

The bricks in the wall behind Kai moved.

They moved away to make a hole in the wall.

The hole was big enough for Kai to climb through. BC followed him.

Kai and BC stood in the battle chamber. Kai looked at the first wall. "Nothing on that wall for a cold place, BC," he said.

Kai went to the middle wall.

"This will be good in an icy land," said Kai. "It shoots three blasts of fire at once!"

T-F-1000

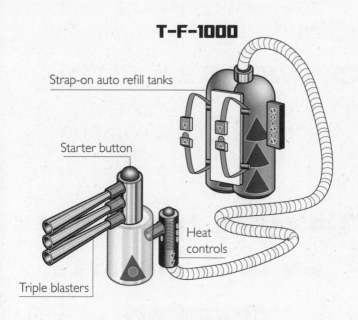

Strap-on auto refill tanks

Starter button

Heat controls

Triple blasters

"That will melt ice," said BC.

"It sure will," said Kai. Then Kai went to take something else.

He heard a noise.

CLUNK GRRR CLUNK

Then he heard a computer voice.

"No more from here. Go to transport chamber. Use slide."

Chapter 3

The lighthouse had a secret
slide. It went from Kai's
bedroom to the lab. Kai used it
at night. It got him from his bed
to the lab fast. The slide went
from the lab to the transport
chamber, too. Kai and BC got
into the slide. They slid down
to the transport chamber.

The Build-a-Ride computer was already on.

"Yes!" said Kai. "We get to build our ride again."

"We'll need to move on ice," said BC. "And it will be very windy."

Kai went to make his ride when he heard

BEEP BEEP

Kai took out his orb.

He looked at the screen.

"It's the BMC," said Kai.
"We have to go under water.
That's how we get to this ice
land."

Kai began to build his ride.
He hit the water button first.

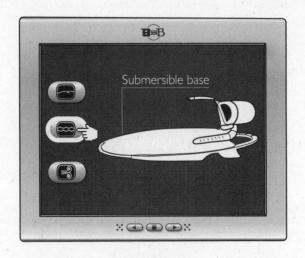

Then he hit the ice button.

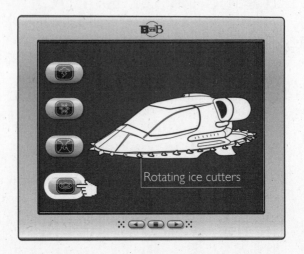

Then he hit see-scope.

Sub mode NOW READY

See above water

Skate mode NOT YET

Stop-ice

"Good," said Kai. "We can go under water and on ice!"

Kai and BC heard a noise behind them. Part of the floor began to move. It was in the middle of the room.

Brrrrrr Brrrrrr

It slid open and left a big space.

Up from the space rose a sub. It was the BG2 Sub-Skate.

The one that Kai had made.

"This is great," said Kai.
"And the cockpit is open.
Let's climb in."

BC jumped into his seat.
Kai climbed in beside him.

Kai looked at the dashboard.
"There's the space for my orb,"
he said.

Kai pushed the orb into its
place. The sub's dashboard lit
up. The cockpit closed.

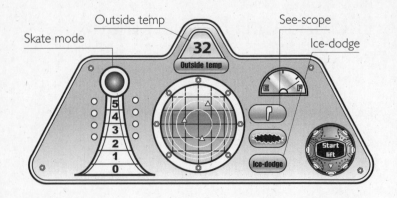

Skate mode · Outside temp · See-scope · Ice-dodge

32
Outside temp

5
4
3
2
1
0

Start
lift

Ice-dodge

"We can't change to Skate yet," said Kai. "We need to win points. The bars will show us when we can change."

"Yes, we will need to fill the bars. Then we can change to skate mode," said BC.

The elevator began to
move. It took Kai and BC
to the top of the lighthouse.
The sub sat on the takeoff pad.
Then Kai's orb beeped.

"We got upgrades, BC,"
said Kai. "Your body has
heat-glow. My hoverboard
has flame-blaster jets.
They'll be good where we
are going."

"Yes, very good," said BC.

Kai keyed in the codes for Isolus on his orb. Then he hit the light button.

The roof of the lighthouse opened. The takeoff pad filled with light. The light shot up into the sky. It took Kai, BC and the sub with it. To the border-land of Isolus.

Chapter 4

The sub splashed down into deep, dark water. The sub's temp screen said –5. "The water out there is very cold, BC," said Kai.

The sub moved quickly. Kai and BC watched the temp drop more and more.

"Now it's −15 and very icy," said Kai. "It's getting hard to drive. There are too many blocks of ice in the water!"

"Not like the water in the water land," said BC.

BC was right. The water-land water had been warm. This was water from an ice land. Kai pushed ice-dodge on the dashboard.

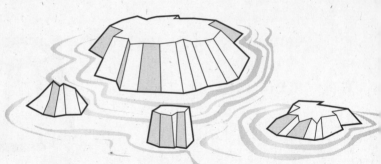

The sub drove through the floating ice.

"This sea has really ugly fish!" said Kai.

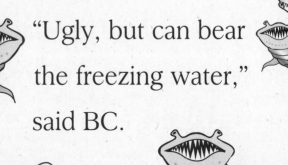

"Ugly, but can bear the freezing water," said BC.

"And there's frozen rot moss," said Kai.

"That stuff eats skin!'

Suddenly the sea was clear. There was no ice floating anywhere. And there were no more ugly fish.

"We're through," said Kai.

"And we won points," said BC.

"We need to win more," said Kai.

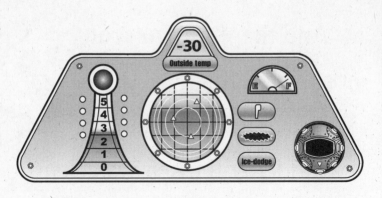

Kai and BC rode on.
"Where is this beast?" asked
Kai. Then the sub's screen
flashed.

Icebergs ahead

Kai looked. In front of him
were two huge icebergs.

There was a very small space between them.

"We won't fit," said BC.

"Yes we will," said Kai.

He turned on the sub's ice cutters.

The ice cutters shot out around the sub. As they hit the ice there was a loud sound.

BRRRRRR
BRRRRRR

The ice cutters cut through the ice. And the sub rode through the space.

"We won more points," said BC. "The bars are full!"

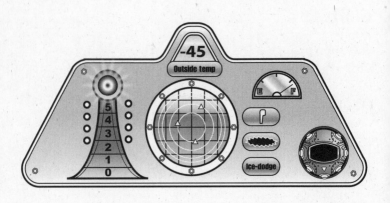

"Good," said Kai. "I'm going to take a look up top."

Kai pushed the button for the see-scope. Then he took a look.

"The ice land is up there, BC," said Kai. "Let's go up. We can then change the sub to skate mode."

Chapter 5

Kai and BC sat on the ice in the skate. "Let's head that way," said Kai. He pointed to hills made of snow and ice.

They were almost there. Then the skate's scanner went off.

Item found

Ride to the left

Kai headed left.
Then he saw it.
Eggshells. Broken egg-
shells. "Something has
hatched here," said Kai.
"And there are tracks.
Big tracks. This beast
has big feet."

They began to follow
the tracks.

Then a snow-
ball flew at them.

It knocked BC off the skate. Kai looked at what had thrown the snow-ball. It was the beast on the card in the lab.

"It's a baby beast," said Kai. "But we know they can be trouble."

"It looks like it's playing in the snow," said BC.

"No," said Kai. "It's been throwing snow-balls at the border-wall."

"We need to stop it," said Kai. "It's getting ready to throw more snow-balls."

Kai bent down to help BC. He pulled him back onto the skate. Suddenly a huge round of snow-balls hit them. The balls covered Kai and BC in snow.

Kai turned the skate's stop-ice on. A spray of salt and water shot out. It came from the back of the skate.

It turned the snow into salty water. And it melted a hole in the snow wall. Kai backed the skate out of the hole.

And then Kai heard a noise.

What is it doing? thought

Kai. There was a huge cloud of snow and ice. "Is it making a snow-storm?" asked Kai.

BC's tail was wagging like crazy. "Beast is changing!" said BC.

Kai grabbed his orb. He watched as the snow-storm grew bigger. Then everything went still. The cloud of snow and ice fell away. And there stood a mega-ice-beast.

Kai took a photo with his orb.
A card popped up on the
screen.

The beast opened its mouth. It was getting ready to blast them.

"Snow-storm attacks!" said Kai. The beast sent a big snow-storm their way.

Chapter 6

Snow and ice flew from the beast's mouth. The snow-storm hit Kai and BC hard. They were covered once more. But this time the pile of snow was huge.

Kai tried the stop-ice again. "There is too much snow," said Kai. "I don't know if this will work."

"The stop-ice isn't enough," said BC. Kai set the skate to turbo charge.

The skate pushed hard against the wall of snow.

"It hasn't done much at all," said Kai. "I'm using too much power. And we are too packed in to use the T-F-1000."

"I can try my heat-glow," said BC.

BC climbed off the skate.

BC pushed his body against the wall of snow. "Now," said BC. Kai pushed the button on the orb.

Heat-glow on

BC's body glowed with heat. BC gave off so much heat, the snow melted.

"You've done it, BC," said Kai. But then another snow-storm hit them.

The snow-storm blew Kai and BC off the skate. Then the beast blew another storm at them. The storm pushed Kai and BC. They landed in the freezing water.

"Are you okay, BC?" asked Kai. "That beast can whip up a huge storm."

"Okay," said BC. "But need to get out of the water."

Kai and BC climbed out of the water. They ran back to the skate. Then Kai saw the beast.

"Oh, no," he said. "I think it's changing again."

Kai took a photo of the beast with his orb. A card popped up.

BEAST I.D.

B vs B

CHILLMAXATAN
Chills and spills!

Strength	★★★★★
Attack Power	★★★★★
Speed	★★★☆☆

The beast had seen them. It lifted its tail. It slammed it down hard on the ice.

The beast turned on Kai and BC. It sent a huge snow- and ice-storm attack toward them.

Let's head up there. We need to stop it from making more snow and ice.

And stop the storms from its mouth!

The beast shook the ice land with its feet and tail. Snow and ice crashed down everywhere.

Everything is caving in.

CCRRRRRRKKK!

The ice shelf is falling down!

Chapter 7

Kai and BC were stuck.

They were under the ice and snow. The beast was throwing ice and snow at the border-wall.

BC was melting some of the ice with his heat-glow. But it wasn't enough.

"I can use the hoverboard's

flame-blaster jets," said Kai.
"You use your eye lasers as
well, BC."

Slowly, they melted the ice
and snow.

Kai and BC stood on the
hoverboard. They both looked
at the beast. It didn't know they
were free.

"I have an idea," said Kai.
"We need to melt that beast.
That will stop it."

"How?" asked BC.

"By using all our heat in the right way," said Kai. "I'll use the T-F-1000 for the mouth-storms. And I'll use the hoverboard jets. They can melt the ice that's under the beast."

"What will I do?" asked BC.

"You get in under its tummy," said Kai. "Then hit it with your heat-glow. Let's do it!"

Kai blasted the beast with heat. The jets turned the ice under the beast to water. The beast began to slide.

BC went in under the beast. He glowed. The beast began to melt. Water rushed away like a fast river. It took what was left of the beast with it. It went far away.

"Beast can't make ice and snow now," said BC.

"No, said Kai. "We've stopped it. It can't break through the wall ever again." Or so Kai thought.

Chapter 8

BC climbed back on the
hoverboard with Kai.

"Time to go?" asked BC.

"You bet," said Kai. "Come
on, Border Guard buddy.
Home time for you and me.
You battled well today, BC.
I think you should have a trip to
the beach!'

"Think I've had enough water today," said BC.

Kai took out his orb. The screen flashed.

"We won upgrades," said Kai. "I hope they will help

us when we go on our next battle."

Kai pushed the button on the orb for home.

A bright light came down from above. It picked up Kai and BC. Then it shot back up. It took Kai and BC with it. Back to the lighthouse.

The border-wall was safe once more. For now.

BEAST BATTLE STATS

CHILLMAXATAN
A real melting moment

Battle Plays	★★★★☆
New Attacks	★★☆☆☆
Energy	★☆☆☆☆

BORDER GUARD BATTLE STATS

Kai Masters

Kai turns up the heat in this battle!

Battle Plays ★★★★★

Upgrades ★★★★★

Border Guard Level

www.boyvsbeast.com

web mode

Games, sneak peeks and more!

Can you beat the Boy vs Beast high score?

BATTLE OF THE WORLDS

Did you miss books 1 to 4?

BATTLE OF THE BORDERS

Have you read them all?